For Amelia – P. R.

For my brother, Rob – C. D.

First published 2002 by Walker Books Ltd
87 Vauxhall Walk, London SE11 5HJ

This edition produced 2003 for
The Book People Ltd, Hall Wood Avenue
Haydock, St Helens WA11 9UL

10 9 8 7 6 5 4 3 2 1

Text © 2002 Phyllis Root
Illustrations © 2002 Christopher Denise

The right of Phyllis Root and Christoper Denise
to be identified as author and illustrator respectively
of this work has been asserted by them in accordance
with the Copyright, Designs and Patents Act 1988

This book has been typeset in Kennerley

Printed in China

British Library Cataloguing in Publication Data:
a catalogue record for this book
is available from the British Library

ISBN 0-7445-8542-2

www.walkerbooks.co.uk

OLiVeR
FiNDS HiS WAY

Phyllis Root

illustrated by

Christopher Denise

TED SMART

While Mother Bear hangs out the washing
and Father Bear rakes the leaves,
Oliver chases a big yellow leaf ...

down the hill,

round a clumpy bush,

under a twisty tree,

and all the way

to the edge of the wood.

Oliver looks for the

yellow leaf.

He can't see it.

Oliver looks for his house.

No house.

Mother Bear? Father Bear?

Oliver thinks,

and he begins to run.

Oliver runs to a tree.

That's not the twisty tree!

He runs to a bush.

That's not the clumpy bush!

All alone at the edge of
the wood,
Oliver starts to cry.
Oliver is lost.

Oliver cries
and cries.

Oliver is still lost.

Oliver rubs his nose
and thinks.

He thinks
and thinks.

Then, all alone at the
edge of the wood,
Oliver has an idea.

"*Roar!*"

"Roar!"

"Roar!"

From far away,
under a twisty tree,
round a clumpy bush,
and all the way up the hill,
Oliver hears Mother Bear
roar back.
Oliver hears Father Bear
roar back.

Oliver runs and runs,
under the twisty tree,

round the clumpy bush,

up the hill,
all the way
to his very own house
with a pile of leaves
and washing on
the line.

All the way to

Mother Bear and Father Bear

who have warm bear hugs ...

just for Oliver.